FIERCE FEMALES OF FICTION

HARLEY QUINN

DC COMICS VILLAIN TURNED HEROINE

KENNY ABDO

abdobooks.com

Published by Abdo Zoom, a division of ABDO, P.O. Box 398166, Minneapolis, Minnesota 55439. Copyright © 2021 by Abdo Consulting Group, Inc. International copyrights reserved in all countries. No part of this book may be reproduced in any form without written permission from the publisher. Fly!™ is a trademark and logo of Abdo Zoom.

Printed in the United States of America, North Mankato, Minnesota.
102020
012021

THIS BOOK CONTAINS RECYCLED MATERIALS

Photo Credits: Alamy, AP Images, Everett Collection, Getty Images, Newscom, Shutterstock, ©Gage Skidmore p9 / CC BY-SA 2.0
Production Contributors: Kenny Abdo, Jennie Forsberg, Grace Hansen
Design Contributors: Dorothy Toth, Neil Klinepier, Laura Graphenteen

Library of Congress Control Number: 2020910911

Publisher's Cataloging-in-Publication Data

Names: Abdo, Kenny, author.
Title: Harley Quinn: DC Comics villain turned heroine / by Kenny Abdo
Other title: DC Comics villain turned heroine
Description: Minneapolis, Minnesota : Abdo Zoom, 2021 | Series: Fierce females of fiction | Includes online resources and index.
Identifiers: ISBN 9781098223113 (lib. bdg.) | ISBN 9781098223816 (ebook) | ISBN 9781098224165 (Read-to-Me ebook)
Subjects: LCSH: Harley Quinn (Fictitious character)--Juvenile literature. | Batman films--Juvenile literature. | Women superheroes--Juvenile literature. | Fierce females of fiction --Juvenile literature. | Heroes--Juvenile literature. | Characters and characteristics in literature--Juvenile literature.
Classification: DDC 809.3--dc23

TABLE OF CONTENTS

Harley Quinn 4

Backstory 8

Journey 14

Epic-Logue 20

Glossary 22

Online Resources 23

Index 24

HARLEY QUINN

Going from respected **psychiatrist** to the deranged Clown Princess of Crime, Harley Quinn makes the dark underworld way more colorful.

Villain turned team leader, Quinn is one of the most popular **anti-heroes** in the DC Universe!

BACKSTORY

Comic book creators Bruce Timm and Paul Dini wanted to introduce a sidekick for the Joker. They named her Harley Quinn. It is a play on the character **Harlequin** from a popular kind of comedy in Italian theaters, *commedia dell'arte*.

A **soap opera** actress named Arleen Sorkin inspired Dini and Timm. During an episode of *Days of Our Lives*, Sorkin dressed as a court **jester** and spoke in a thick Northeastern accent.

Quinn's first appearance was in *Batman: The Animated Series*. During the episode "Joker's Favor," Quinn was introduced as the villain's loyal helper.

JOURNEY

Dr. Harleen Quinzel was a brilliant **psychiatrist** at the Arkham Asylum. She was assigned the Joker as her patient. Quinzel eventually fell in love with him. They then became partners in crime.

Dr. Quinzel became Harley Quinn when Batman put the Joker back in Arkham. Quinn broke the Joker out, kicking off their crime spree.

Quinn uses many weapons. She wields her **iconic** baseball bat and giant mallet in most fights.

Though often working solo, Quinn has joined forces with a few teams. Quinn, along with Catwoman and Poison Ivy, formed the Gotham City Sirens.

Quinn was not only **recruited** by the Suicide Squad, she became its leader.

This team of "villains" takes on high-risk secret missions that no one else is crazy enough to do.

EPIC-LOGUE

Seventeen actors have played Quinn over time. Arleen Sorkin voiced Quinn for more than 20 years. Margot Robbie most famously portrayed her in two DC Universe films.

From hardcore criminal to hero, Quinn is a character that is no joke.

GLOSSARY

anti-hero – a character in a story who is unlike a regular hero that the audience still roots for.

harlequin – a character used in certain stories for comic relief, usually dressed in a diamond-patterned costume.

iconic – widely known and recognized for its unique features.

jester – an entertainer from the medieval and Renaissance era.

psychiatrist – a doctor who specializes in identifying and treating mental illness.

recruit – someone brought into a group or team for their skills.

soap opera – a television drama series dealing with daily events in the lives of a group of characters.

ONLINE RESOURCES

Booklinks
NONFICTION NETWORK
FREE! ONLINE NONFICTION RESOURCES

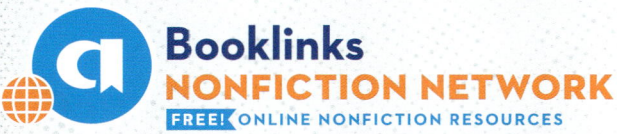

To learn more about Harley Quinn, please visit **abdobooklinks.com** or scan this QR code. These links are routinely monitored and updated to provide the most current information available.

INDEX

Batman (character) 15

Batman: The Animated Series (show) 12

Catwoman (character) 17

commedia dell'arte 9

Days of Our Lives (show) 10

DC Universe 6, 20

Dini, Paul 9, 10

Joker (character) 9, 12, 14, 15

Poison Ivy (character) 17

Robbie, Margot 20

Sorkin, Arleen 10, 20

Suicide Squad (team) 18, 19

Timm, Bruce 9, 10

weapons 16